SCOOBY-DOO! and YOU:
A Collect the Clues Mystery
THE CASE OF THE TELEVISION MONSTER

By James Gelsey

WORLDWIDE PUBLISHING™

SCHOLASTIC INC.

New York Toronto London Auckland Sydney
Mexico City New Delhi Hong Kong

ISBN 0-439-23159-0

12 11 10 9 8 7 6 5 4 3   2 3 4 5 6/0

Cover and interior illustrations by Duendes del Sur
Cover and interior design by Madalina Stefan

Printed in the U.S.A.

First Scholastic printing, April 2001

SCOOBY-DOO! and YOU:

A Collect the Clues Mystery

THE CASE OF THE TELEVISION MONSTER

It's a beautiful, sunny day, and you're on your way to Patty's Pancakes for lunch. You don't usually have pancakes for lunch, but then you don't usually meet Scooby-Doo and his friends for lunch, either. So you're willing to make an exception because you know it'll be worth it.

Even though you've never been there before, you recognize the restaurant right away. It's shaped like a stack of pancakes — a really, really big stack of pancakes. The Mystery, Inc. gang is waiting outside for you.

"Hey!" Fred calls. "You made it!"

"Let's get inside," Shaggy says. "Scooby and I are, like, starved."

You smile because you know Scooby and Shaggy are *always* starved.

Inside, you follow the gang to a booth and sit down. A waitress hands you very large menus. "Man, I've never seen so many kinds of pancakes before," Shaggy gasps. "Look at this, Scoob. They've even got coconut cream pie pancakes!"

"*Rechhh!*" Scooby says.

"How about chocolate-covered pretzel and peanut butter pancakes?" Shaggy suggests.

Scooby thinks about it for a minute and then shakes his head.

"Scooby, there are, like, over a hundred different kinds of pancakes here," Shaggy says. "There's *gotta* be one kind you like."

"*Ruh-uh,*" he says.

"Well, what kind of pancakes do you want, Scooby?" asks Daphne.

"*Rooby rack rancakes!*" says Scooby with a great big smile.

"Very funny, Scooby," Velma says. "But I don't think they can make Scooby Snack pancakes. Maybe we should just ask the waitress for a suggestion. "

The waitress walks over and Fred asks what she recommends.

"Well, that food critic guy on channel three just loves our blueberry and honey walnut pancakes," the waitress says.

"Oh, no," Shaggy says. "I'm not eating anything that has to do with anyone on TV."

Daphne sees the puzzled look on your face.

"Don't listen to Shaggy," she says. "He's still a little spooked from our last mystery. It took place at a television station."

"It was a pretty tough mystery, too," Fred adds. "We really could have used your help."

"I have an idea," Velma says. "Why don't you read our Clue Keeper and see if you can solve it yourself?"

You nod your head with excitement. "That'd be great!" you exclaim.

Daphne opens her pocketbook and hands you a small notebook.

"Here it is," she says. "I think I took pretty

good notes. But just in case, we've added a few things to help you along."

"When you see this sign , that means you've just met a suspect," Velma explains. "And a shows you've found a clue."

"We'll even ask you some questions along the way to help you organize your notes in your own Clue Keeper," Fred offers.

"May I take your order?" the waitress asks.

Everyone looks over and sees that Shaggy and Scooby aren't even close to making a decision.

"But, Scoob, if we get the chocolate chip and banana pancakes, we may not have room for the praline crunch and watermelon pancakes," Shaggy says.

"We need a few more minutes, please," Daphne tells the waitress.

"Take your time," Velma says to you. "It looks like we're going to be here for a while."

You open the Clue Keeper and start to read *The Case of the Television Monster*.

Clue Keeper Entry 1

Digby Rostow, the owner of channel eight, had invited us to his television station. My uncle is a friend of his and suggested that Mr. Rostow call us when he started receiving mysterious letters.

The station owner took my uncle's advice. He phoned and told us he was worried someone was going to cause trouble at the television station.

When we arrived, the receptionist sent us right to Mr. Rostow's office. We walked down a hallway with a glass wall. The wall looked out over all of the television studios at channel eight. One was set up for the news and another was arranged for a cooking show. There was even a set that looked like a giant playroom. In it, a man wearing a suit and tie danced around with a broom.

When we got to Mr. Rostow's office, his door was wide open. It was hard not to overhear the argument going on inside.

"I don't care how much you're offering, I'm still not selling the station," Mr. Rostow said angrily.

"I just now looked at the *Channel Eight News* set, Digby. Do you really think that new furniture will help your ratings?" a man replied.

"How I run this station is my business, not yours, Whitman," Mr. Rostow replied. "I'd rather go off the air than sell to you."

"Suit yourself, Digby," the man said as he left. "But I'll find a way to get this station, with or without your consent." The man stormed out of the office and marched right past us. 👁👁

"Hey, that was W.P. Whitman," Fred said. "You know, the guy who owns *The Daily Bulletin.*"

"That's right," said Mr. Rostow as he came out of his office.

"Why does he want to buy your TV station?" Velma asked.

"So he can make even more money and control all of the news in this town," Mr. Rostow replied bitterly. "But you don't have to worry yourselves about that. I'm really glad you could come." He glanced at his

wristwatch and frowned. "Oh, boy, it's already started. Come on in, kids."

Mr. Rostow walked back into his office and turned on a television set.

"Hey, it's the guy we just saw dancing!" Shaggy said.

"That's Sam Silly, and you're watching the very first episode of *The Sam Silly Show*," Mr. Rostow said. "I think it will be a ratings blockbuster, and we desperately need one. The station hasn't been doing very well lately. If the mysterious threats I told you about don't stop, and if our ratings don't go up, I may have to sell the station to W.P. Whitman after all."

"Like, by ratings, do you mean the number of people who watch your channel?" Shaggy asked.

"Exactly," Mr. Rostow confirmed. "If you don't have good ratings companies won't advertise on your channel. The money from advertising commercials is what pays for the programs at TV stations. A bad rating means fewer commercials. Fewer commercials means we can't pay to keep our programs on the air."

"Is there a reason you want us to see this show?" I asked.

"Yes. The last threatening message I received on my phone machine said I'd see that the caller wasn't kidding when I tuned in to the first episode of *Sam Silly*. You can imagine how worried I am right now."

Mr. Rostow raised the volume and sat down behind his desk. We all turned our attention toward the TV set.

Sam Silly started juggling a bowling ball, a picture frame, and a cat. A doorbell rang on the show and Sam Silly dropped what he was juggling. The bowling ball landed on his foot, so he hopped over to the playroom door.

"I'll bet it's Mailman Moe," Sam Silly said in a very comical, high-pitched voice. He opened the door and . . .

Sam Silly jumped back, looking terrified.

A strange creature burst into the room. It had a small television set for a head and its

body was wound up in thin, shiny black ribbon. Its eyes glowed eerily, as if two blank, greenish TV lights shown from the sockets.

"Jinkies!" Velma gasped. "I don't think that's Mailman Moe. He's some kind of mummy wrapped up in videotape!"

"People of channel eight, beware!" the monster warned in a low, growly voice. "The curse of the Television Monster has begun. I will haunt every show on this station until channel eight goes off the air forever!"

The monster let out a maniacal laugh.

Sam Silly was *scared* silly and ran right

out through the playroom door. The monster followed him out the door.

Mr. Rostow snapped up his phone, pushed a red button, and shouted, "Go to commercial! Go to commercial!"

The television screen went black and then a commercial started.

"Excuse me, kids, I need to go," Mr. Rostow said. "I'll catch up with you later. If you need anything, ask my assistant, Ben."

Mr. Rostow ran out of his office. We went back into the hallway overlooking the studios. Looking down through the glass, I thought I saw something dart quickly around the desks in the news studio.

"Did you just see something dash through the news studio?" I asked the gang.

"The only thing Scooby and I want to see is the exit," Shaggy said.

"Hmm," said Velma. "I'll bet there's more to this Television Monster than meets the eye."

"Well, gang, that's why we're here," Fred said.

"I was afraid you were going to say that," groaned Shaggy.

"**W**ell, it looks like there's a mystery brewing. And I think we found our first suspect. Take out your Clue Keeper and a pen or pencil. Then answer these questions about the suspect you just met."

1. What is the suspect's name?

2. Why is he at the television station?

3. What does he want that makes him a suspect?

"Once you're done, read the next entry to see where we went next."

Clue Keeper Entry 2

We stood in the hallway trying to decide where we should go first.

"How about the cafeteria?" Shaggy suggested. "I'll bet they serve the leftovers from all those cooking shows."

Scooby licked his lips and rubbed his stomach in anticipation.

"Why don't we look around the television studios, instead?" Fred said.

"Good idea, Fred," Velma agreed.

"No way!" Shaggy said. "What if we run into that creepy monster we just saw?"

"What creepy monster?" asked a voice

from behind us. We turned around and saw someone holding a huge stack of videotapes. The pile was so high, in fact, it stopped just under the man's nose.

"The one on *The Sam Silly Show*," Velma replied.

"I don't remember there being any monster on *The Sam Silly Show*," he said. The man suddenly sneezed and dropped the stack of videotapes. They crashed to the floor.

Without the videos in front of him, we saw that the man wasn't much older than we are.

"*Gesundheit,*" I said. "Can we give you a hand?" Fred, Velma, Shaggy, and I each picked up a couple of videotapes.

"Thanks," he replied. "I'm Ben. Ben Frazier. I'm not usually this clumsy, but I hurt my hand doing some work on the news set earlier today."

"Are you the same Ben who's Mr. Rostow's assistant?" Velma asked.

"Mr. Rostow's *gofer* is more like it," Ben replied.

Shaggy laughed. "As in *go for this, and go for that*?" he asked.

"Exactly right!" Ben confirmed. "I was supposed to work in the news department, but so far all I've done is move furniture, get coffee, deliver videotapes, and photocopy scripts. Not exactly the exciting world of television that Mr. Rostow promised."

"All those things sound important," I said.

"Maybe, but they're nowhere near as important as being a television anchorman," Ben continued. "That's what I really want to be. If I could only break open an important news story, I know that Mr. Rostow would give me a shot at the news. But for now, I'm stuck carrying videotapes. Well, I'd better be going now. I have to deliver some of these videos to Wellington Weiss."

"Do you mean Wellington Weiss, the talk show host of *The Wellington Weiss Show*?" I asked.

"That's him," Ben replied.

"Boy, wouldn't it be groovy to meet an actual TV star?" I wondered out loud. "I used to love *The Wellington Weiss Show*. I felt sad that they took it off the air."

"Most shows get canceled sooner or later," Velma commented.

"I know," I admitted. "I'd love to meet Wellington Weiss, even if he isn't on TV anymore."

"We can give you a hand bringing these videotapes to him," Fred offered.

"And while you're doing that, Scooby and I can find the cafeteria," Shaggy suggested. "All this standing around and talking about videotapes has made us hungry."

"Since when do videotapes make you hungry?" Velma asked.

"They don't," Shaggy explained. "But standing around talking does. We'll catch up with you later. Come on, Scoob."

"All right, but stay out of trouble," I warned.

"What kind of trouble could we get into in a television station?" Shaggy asked.

"We don't want to find out!" Fred answered.

"So, I'll bet you noticed the 👀 on page 17, right? That means it's time for you to open up your Clue Keeper. Answer these questions about the possible suspect you've just met. When you're done, read the next entry in our Clue Keeper to see who we met up with next."

1. What is the suspect's name?

2 What is his job at the television station?

3. What does he want to do that makes him a suspect?

21

Clue Keeper Entry 3

We helped Ben carry the videotapes to Wellington Weiss's dressing room. As we got closer, we suddenly heard a man yell for help.

"That sounds like Mr. Weiss!" Ben exclaimed. He ran down the hallway to Wellington Weiss's dressing room. By the time we got there, the door was open and Ben was already inside. The dressing room was very plain. There was a sofa and coffee table on one side. A long makeup table and mirror lined the other wall.

"Is everything all right?" Fred asked.

"Yes, yes, fine, fine," answered a man sitting on the sofa. It was Wellington Weiss, the former TV talk show host. He held a glass of water in one hand and a white handkerchief over his forehead with the other.

"What happened?" asked Velma.

"Mr. Weiss says that —" Ben began.

"I can speak for myself, thank you," Wellington Weiss said in a very familiar voice. "I was in my dressing room when I heard a strange sound in the hallway. I opened my door and saw some kind of . . . of . . . *creature* with a television for a head! He made some growling noise, knocked me over, and then ran out into the stairwell."

"Excuse me, Mr. Weiss, but I have to get some tapes to the control room for the evening news," Ben interrupted.

"Yes, yes, of course, Ben," Mr. Weiss said. "On your way out, you can take those tapes on the table back to the video library. I'm sorry to say my VCR at home ate one of them again. Most of the pieces are still in one of the boxes, but they do seem to get everywhere."

Ben gathered the tapes and then nodded good-bye. "See you later. And thanks again for your help."

"This really is quite an honor, Mr. Weiss," I said. "I used to love your show."

"Why, thank you, young lady, that's very flattering," he replied. "You know, my show had the highest ratings ever and helped build this television station. But then Digby Rostow decided to cancel it, leaving me a man without a show. Now I spend my time walking around the TV studios, seeking inspiration."

Mr. Weiss leaned forward and lowered his voice. "I'm trying to develop an idea for a new show, you see. My new show will shoot right to the top of the ratings. And I won't give my brilliant new idea to channel eight. I'll be a star on a new station. Yes, yes, I'm going to make Digby Rostow sorry he ever took Wellington Weiss off the air."

"Well, good luck, Mr. Weiss," Fred said. "We have to go find our friends now."

"It was a pleasure meeting you, sir," I said. "And whenever you do that new show, you can bet we'll be watching."

"That's very kind, young lady," Mr. Weiss said. "Yes, yes."

We left Wellington Weiss and walked back down the hallway. I looked through the glass wall and — once again — I saw something moving in the news studio.

"I don't believe it," I said with a smile.

We all saw Shaggy and Scooby sitting at

the anchor desk. They were pretending to be doing a newscast.

"They're going to get us thrown out of here. We'd better go get them," Fred said. "And quickly!"

Velma's Mystery-Solving Tips

"It looks like we've found another suspect, right? Check out the 👀 on page 23 to make sure you found him. Then answer these questions in your Clue Keeper."

1. What is the suspect's name?

2. What is his relationship to the television station?

3. What does he want that makes him a suspect?

"Once you've finished jotting down your notes, read the next entry to see what happened to us next."

Clue Keeper Entry 4

Fred, Daphne, and I raced down to the television studio. We arrived just as Shaggy and Scooby walked off the set.

"Shaggy! Scooby! What were you doing?" I called.

"Don't worry, Daphne," Mr. Rostow said. "They were giving us a hand."

"*Rand a raw,*" Scooby said, holding up his front paw. He and Shaggy giggled.

"We needed someone to sit behind the new desk so we could get the lighting just right," Mr. Rostow explained. "Shaggy and

Scooby volunteered — in exchange for a visit to the cafeteria, that is."

Shaggy and Scooby smiled.

Suddenly, the studio started buzzing with activity. Morton O'Malley, the anchorman, walked onto the set and sat down behind the news desk. A technician handed him a clip-on microphone and his news script.

"Places, everyone," a voice called over the loudspeaker. Morton O'Malley straightened up and looked right into the camera. We could see him on the TV monitors that were hanging all over the studio.

"Good evening. I'm Morton O'Malley," he said. "Tonight's big story: A sudden hailstorm is expected to pelt our town tonight. For more, let's go to our weather map." The picture on the television monitor switched from the news desk to a big weather map.

Suddenly, something burst through the weather map on the wall!

"Zoinks!" Shaggy exclaimed. "It's the Television Monster!"

"The curse of the Television Monster continues!" shouted the creature.

Morton O'Malley sprang to his feet. The monster lunged toward him. He grabbed the newsman by the hair.

"Hey!" Morton O'Malley yelled as the monster gave a swift tug.

The man's hair flew off his head.

"Yikes!" Fred cried.

The monster had yanked off the anchorman's wig. Suddenly bald, Morton O'Malley jumped out of his seat and ran screaming off the set.

"Who's going to be my next victim?" the monster asked, looking straight into the camera. "Stay tuned and find out!" The monster roared and then turned and ran out of the studio.

"After him!" Fred yelled. We all ran out into the hallway, but the Television Monster had disappeared.

"Go to commercial!" Mr. Rostow yelled. "Then get someone to finish the news in studio three."

"Studio three's set up for *Cooking With Wendy*," said Ben as he walked into the studio. "I suggest you use studio four." All the technicians quickly ran out of the news studio, heading for studio four.

"This monster is going to ruin me for sure," Mr. Rostow sighed. "Maybe we *should* just go off the air forever."

"Don't make any quick decisions, Mr. Rostow," Ben said.

"That's right," Fred added. "We're here to help. You figure out a way to stay on the air for now. We'll take care of the rest!"

We moved off to the side while everyone left for studio four.

"Gang, if we're going to help Mr. Rostow save the station, we'd better act fast," Fred said. "Let's start by taking a look around the news set."

Velma walked over to the broken weather map on the floor. She reached down and picked up a piece.

"That monster must be really strong to break through a wall like that," I said.

"Not necessarily," Velma said. "The weather map is mounted on some kind of

Styrofoam board. Even Shaggy could break through it. Hmm, this is peculiar."

"What is it, Velma?" Fred asked.

"Look how straight this side of the piece is," Velma said. "In fact, all of the pieces have straight, clean edges. It looks to me like someone pre-cut the map so it would break apart easily."

"Which means that the Television Monster came to the news set earlier today," Fred said.

"I think we just found our first clue," Velma said.

"You're right, Velma," Fred agreed. "And if we're going to find any more, we'd better split up."

"Like, did you notice the ➤ on page 34? That shows you our first clue. Now open up your Clue Keeper and answer these questions about it."

1. What is the clue?

2. What does it have to do with the Television Monster?

3. Which of the suspects do you think could have left this clue?

"Once you're done, put away your Clue Keeper and read on to see what we found next."

Clue Keeper Entry 5

"Shaggy, you and Scooby come with me," I said. "I want to check out the stairwell where Mr. Weiss saw the monster disappear earlier."

"Good idea, Daphne," Fred said. "Velma and I will finish looking around here and then check out the other studios."

"Let's meet back in Mr. Rostow's office," Velma said.

"Come on, fellas," I said to Shaggy and Scooby.

"Do we have to, Daphne?" Shaggy whined. "Like, Scooby and I are still hungry."

"The sooner we get to the bottom of this mystery, the sooner you can eat," I replied.

The three of us left the studio. We headed back to the hallway outside Wellington Weiss's dressing room and found the door to the stairwell.

Just as I opened the door, something caught my eye on the floor outside Mr. Weiss's dressing room. I walked over — but before I could pick it up — Mr. Weiss's door opened.

"Can I help you, young lady?" Mr. Weiss asked.

"Uh, no, sir," I said. "We were just —"

"— looking for the cafeteria," Shaggy jumped in.

"I was on my way downstairs, as well," Mr. Weiss said. "Care to join me?"

"*Rou ret!*" Scooby said happily.

"He means, 'no thanks,'" I said, giving Scooby a stern look.

"Very well," Mr. Weiss said. He stepped out of his dressing room and closed the door behind him. He pulled a baseball cap over his head. "Can't be too careful with that horrid Television Monster running around. Poor Morton."

We watched Mr. Weiss walk into the stairwell. When he was gone, I picked up the object from the floor.

"It looks like a piece of videotape," I said.

"That's nice, Daph," Shaggy said.

Just then, the stairwell door opened again. Ben Frazier walked out into the hallway. He carried a bag over his shoulder and headed for Mr. Weiss's dressing room.

"He's not there, Ben," I said. "He went to the cafeteria."

"Really? Thanks," Ben said. "I have to get him these tapes before he leaves. See ya later."

"At least we know there's no Television Monster on those stairs now," I said to reassure Shaggy and Scooby. "Let's go."

Shaggy, Scooby, and I walked into the stairwell and found two staircases. One staircase went down and another went up. The door to the stairwell then closed behind us with a click.

"Zoinks! Wh-what was that?" Shaggy asked.

"The door closing," I said. "See?" I turned

and saw something stuck under the door. It was another piece of videotape. In fact, there were a few pieces on the stairs going down.

"Hmm, I think this trail of videotape is more than a coincidence," I said. "We'd better go find Fred and Velma."

"Man, our stomachs can't take much more of this," Shaggy said. "Scooby and I are going downstairs to the cafeteria to get something to eat for real this time."

"All right, you two," I said. "We'll meet you down there."

I put both pieces of videotape in my pocket and started walking up the stairs. At the next stairwell, I opened the door and found myself in the hallway outside Mr. Rostow's office. Fred and Velma were already there.

"Fred, Velma, am I glad to see you," I said. "Did you find any clues?"

"We didn't have any luck," Velma said. "Whoever is behind this mystery is doing a pretty good job of covering his tracks."

"Maybe he's not doing as good a job as he thinks," I said. I showed them the pieces of videotape I'd found and told them about my meeting with Wellington Weiss.

"Sounds like we're getting closer to solving this mystery," Fred said. "Let's find Shaggy and Scooby so we can regroup and plan our next steps."

"That clue on page 38 was a pretty easy one to miss. We're really lucky I spotted it. Take out your Clue Keeper and answer these questions about it."

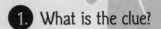

1. What is the clue?

2. What does it have to do with the Television Monster?

3. Who could have left that clue on the stairs?

"After you've had a chance to think about the clue, read my next entry to see what ended up happening next."

Clue Keeper Entry 6

Fred, Velma, and I walked down two flights
of stairs to the cafeteria level. When we got
there, the door was open. We walked the
hallway looking for Shaggy and Scooby.

"Scooby-Doo, where are you?" shouted
Velma.

We heard the muffled sound of two
voices. We followed the sound to a door on
the left side of the hallway. Fred reached out
for the doorknob and quickly pulled the
door open.

"Ahhhhhhh!" screamed Shaggy from inside. Then he stopped, looked at us, and

smiled. "Oh, it's you. Like, we thought you were the Television Monster."

"What are you two doing in this closet?" I asked. "I thought you were going to the cafeteria."

"The cafeteria is at the end of this hall, but we never made it that far," Shaggy explained. "Scooby-Doo and I were on our way when we heard that Television Monster's creepy voice. We decided to play it safe and hide in here."

I noticed an open door next to the closet. "Maybe he ducked in here," I suggested in a whisper. Carefully, we pushed the door open wider and peered inside. Looking around the room, we saw lots of television equipment.

"This must be where they repair the television cameras," Velma said.

"Televisions, too," Shaggy said. "Check out that groovy number."

Shaggy pointed to a golden television sitting on a table in the corner. It must have been very old, because it still had dials for changing the channel.

"Hey, look at this," Fred said. He was reading a piece of paper taped to the top of the television. "It's a work order, dated last Tuesday. I guess this television is really badly broken."

"Whose is it?" I asked.

Fred looked at the paper again. "You're not going to believe it," he said. We all looked at the paper. In the space where a name was supposed to go, we saw only two letters written: *W.W.*

"Of course," I said. "It all makes sense now."

"What does?" asked Shaggy.

"If you ask me, our monster's next television appearance is about to be canceled," Velma said.

"And how do you cancel a monster?" asked Shaggy.

"Easy," Fred said. "You set a trap."

"I'm sorry I asked," Shaggy replied.

"And we're going to need your help and Scooby's," Fred added.

"Now I'm *really* sorry I asked," Shaggy said.

"How about it?" I said to Scooby. "Are you ready to be the bravest dog in the whole world?"

"*Ruh-uh,*" Scooby said, shaking his head.

"How about for a Scooby Snack?" I offered.

Scooby thought for a moment.

"*Rokay!*" he barked. I gave Scooby his Scooby Snack and he gobbled it down in a flash.

"Velma, you get Mr. Rostow and bring him to the control room. We're going to need

his help," Fred said. "The Television Monster won't be able to pass up an opportunity to ruin a TV show. So let's go to studio three and get ourselves set up."

"Set up for what?" Shaggy asked.

"You'll see," Fred said with a smile.

Clue Keeper Entry 8

We walked down the hallway and went inside studio three.

"Scooby, like, do you see what I see?" asked Shaggy.

"*Reah!*" Scooby replied with a smile.

The studio was set up for *Cooking With Wendy*. A long counter stood along the front. An electric mixer and some mixing bowls were already out. A double oven, a large food pantry, an enormous refrigerator, and a sink lined the wall behind the counter. A fake kitchen door stood on the right side.

"Okay, here's the plan," Fred said. "Scooby, you'll pretend to be doing a cooking show. Shaggy, you hide in the food pantry. I'll be hiding just offstage, over there. Daphne, you pretend to operate the camera. When the Television Monster shows up, I'll give the signal. Shaggy will jump out of the pantry and grab the monster. Velma and I will run on and tie him up with one of the microphone cords."

"And what should I do?" boomed Mr. Rostow's voice from the control room.

"Make it look like we're on the air," Fred called back. "Places, everyone!"

"You heard the man, Scoob," Shaggy said. "To the kitchen."

"*Roo ruh ritchen!*" Scooby echoed happily.

Shaggy and Scooby walked onto the kitchen set. Shaggy opened the pantry door and found an apron and a chef's hat hanging inside the door. He tied the apron around Scooby and then put the chef's hat on Scooby's head.

"Gee, Scoob, you look just like a famous chef," Shaggy said.

"*Rich run?*" asked Scooby.

"Like, Chef Dog-ar-dee," Shaggy joked as he stepped into the pantry. "Hey, it's dark in here."

"Then keep the door open a little," called Fred. "And remember not to make any noise. We don't want the Television Monster to know you're in there. Daphne, start the camera. We're ready, Mr. Rostow."

I found the button that turned on the television camera. Scooby's picture ap-

peared on the television monitors hanging in the studio.

He grabbed a mixing bowl and put it in front of him. He got some milk and eggs from the refrigerator. He opened the pantry and Shaggy handed him the flour and sugar. Scooby whistled as he put all the ingredients into the mixing bowl. He put the bowl onto the electric mixer and turned it on. Suddenly, the Television Monster burst through the kitchen door.

"The curse of the Television Monster strikes again!" the monster cried as he walked menacingly toward Scooby.

"Now!" Fred called from offstage, but nothing happened. "I said, 'Now!'"

Scooby opened the pantry door. Shaggy was sitting with a mouthful of cookies and an empty box on his lap. He shrugged and then reached up and pulled the pantry door closed.

Scooby backed away from the monster and accidentally bumped into the mixer, putting it on high. The mixing bowl spun around furiously, spewing bits of cake batter everywhere.

Scooby tried to run — but he slipped on some batter that splattered on the floor.

The Television Monster was about to grab Scooby!

But a huge glob of batter suddenly landed on the monster's television face!

Unable to see, the monster flailed his arms as he tried to grab the counter. One of the strands of videotape hanging from his body got caught in the mixer blades. The

blades were still turning! The Television Monster began to spin so fast that he fell to the floor.

"Come on," Fred said, stepping forward. "Let's see who this Television Monster really is!"

"It's a pretty good mystery, isn't it?" asks Daphne as you put down the Clue Keeper. "And I'll bet you've already got an idea of who was wearing the Television Monster costume."

"But just to be sure, take out your Clue Keeper and look over your notes," Fred suggests.

"Compare your list of suspects with the list of clues," Velma says. "And try to figure out which suspects could have left each of the clues. Only one of the suspects will be somehow connected to both of the clues."

"And since Shaggy and Scooby are still arguing over what kind of pancakes they want, take your time," Daphne says. "When you've solved the mystery, turn the page and see who was really under all that video-tape."

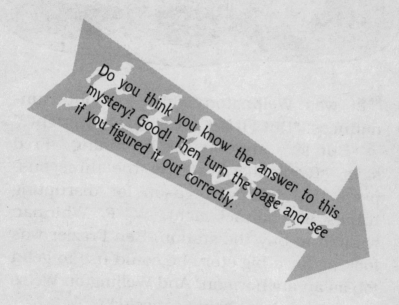

Do you think you know the answer to this mystery? Good! Then turn the page and see if you figured it out correctly.

"It was Wellington Weiss!" Daphne announces. "But I'll bet you knew that, right?"

"But let's start at the beginning," Fred says. "Remember, each of the three suspects had his own reason for disrupting things at channel eight. W. P. Whitman wanted to buy the station. Ben Frazier was looking for a big story he could use to get a job as an anchorman. And Wellington Weiss was angry about being canceled."

"The first clue we found was the pre-cut

weather map that the monster burst through," Velma says. "And each of the suspects visited the news set earlier that day. Mr. Whitman went to look at the furniture. Ben told us he was doing work on the set. And Mr. Weiss went for a walk to get ideas for his new show."

"Our second clue eliminated W. P. Whitman," Daphne explains. "Because only Ben and Mr. Weiss had access to a lot of videotape. Ben Frazier told us he spent some time repairing broken videotapes. And Mr. Weiss mentioned that his VCR at home kept eating the tapes, leaving pieces everywhere."

"But it was the last clue that singled out Wellington Weiss," Velma says. "You'll remember that we found his television in the repair room downstairs. That means he didn't have a TV in his dressing room. He even said he had to watch the tapes at home."

"And since he didn't have a TV in his dressing room," Daphne says, "there's no way he could ever have known that the

Television Monster yanked off Morton O'Malley's wig on the news broadcast."

"He knew about it because he *was* the Television Monster," Fred says. "He later admitted that it was all part of his idea for a new TV show about a monster trying to take over a TV station."

"A show he could star in, of course," adds Velma.

"The funny thing is that the ratings that night skyrocketed," Fred chuckles. "Mr. Weiss created ratings success for the station."

"It's just too bad he did it in such a nasty way," Daphne says. "But all in all, that was a pretty groovy mystery, wasn't it?"

You nod your head in agreement as the waitress returns.

"Are you ready yet?" she asks Shaggy and Scooby.

"Yes," Shaggy replies. "We'll each have an order of plain pancakes."

"Plain pancakes!" Fred exclaims. "But there are over a hundred different kinds."

"I know, but it's too hard to pick just one," Shaggy says. "So we decided to keep it simple."

"Two orders of plain pancakes," the waitress repeats. "What kind of syrup would you like?"

"Huh?" asks Scooby.

The waitress reaches across and turns over the menu.

"You get to choose the kind of syrup you

want from our list of sixty-three different kinds," she says.

"Oh, brother," Velma moans. "Here we go again."

"*Rooby-rooby-roo!*" barks Scooby.